找回注意力

文／孟瑛如、周文聿
圖／朱惠甄
英文翻譯／吳侑達

U0065242

我從小就像身上裝了馬達一般，總是沒定性。

討厭需要輪流或等待的活動。

任何情境，我都可以過度的跑來跑去或爬上爬下，很強吧！

上課的時候，我可以有橡皮擦玩橡皮擦，有手指玩手指，常弄丟上課或活動的必要物品。生活的三分之二時間都花在找東西和想辦法集中注意力上！很酷吧！

我ㄨㄛˇ屬ㄕㄨˇ狗ㄍㄡˇ，
媽ㄇㄚ媽ㄇㄚ叫ㄐㄧㄠˋ我ㄨㄛˇ
跳ㄊㄧㄠˋ跳ㄊㄧㄠˋ狗ㄍㄡˇ！

每次有事，老師
都把我請出教室，
所以我跟輔導老師
很熟！

支持

正向

食物

運動

醫療

輔ㄈㄨˇ導ㄉㄠˇ老ㄌㄠˇ師ㄕ
教ㄐㄧㄠˋ我ㄨㄛˇ不ㄅㄨˋ要ㄧㄠˋ讓ㄖㄤˋ旁ㄆㄤˊ
邊ㄅㄧㄢ的ㄉㄜ事ㄕˋ物ㄨˋ改ㄍㄞˇ變ㄅㄧㄢˋ享ㄒㄧㄤˇ
受ㄕㄡˋ學ㄒㄩㄝˊ習ㄒㄧ的ㄉㄜ初ㄔㄨ衷ㄓㄨㄥ。要ㄧㄠˋ
用ㄩㄥˋ醫ㄧ療ㄌㄧㄠˊ介ㄐㄧㄝˋ入ㄖㄨˋ、固ㄍㄨˋ定ㄉㄧㄥˋ運ㄩㄣˋ
動ㄉㄨㄥˋ、吃ㄔ對ㄉㄨㄟˋ的ㄉㄜ食ㄕˊ物ㄨˋ和ㄏㄜˊ正ㄓㄥˋ
向ㄒㄧㄤˋ支ㄓ持ㄔˊ法ㄈㄚˇ來ㄌㄞˊ找ㄓㄠˇ回ㄏㄨㄟˊ注ㄓㄨˋ意ㄧˋ力ㄌㄧˋ，
捍ㄏㄢˋ衛ㄨㄟˋ自ㄗˋ己ㄐㄧˇ的ㄉㄜ
上ㄕㄤˋ課ㄎㄜˋ權ㄑㄩㄢˊ！

我要上課權，所以開始持續看醫院的兒童心智科。我猜自己的心智會變強！

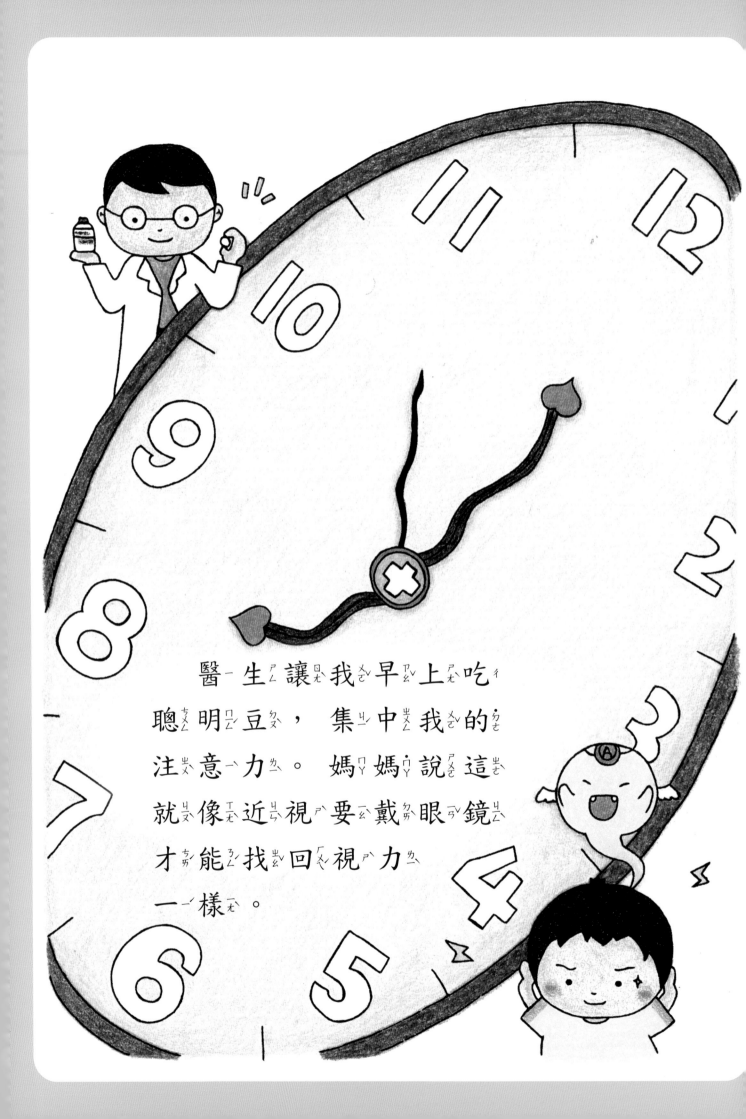

醫生讓我早上吃聰明豆，集中我的注意力。媽媽說這就像近視要戴眼鏡才能找回視力一樣。

吃了聰明豆會有點吃不下午餐，所以媽媽都會在晚飯或消夜時多準備一些東西給我吃！還是一樣好好吃！

老師要我養成早上運動的習慣，要在早上，要有氧及規律，要腦力及體力兼備！

早上運動可以讓我找回上課的注意力，下午運動會變成晚上看連續劇比較專心！哈哈哈！

食物要吃對， 才能找回注意力！

請ㄑ一ㄥˇ用ㄩㄥˋ簡ㄐ一ㄢˇ單ㄉㄢ、 正ㄓㄥˋ向ㄒ一ㄤˋ、 清ㄑ一ㄥ楚ㄔㄨˇ、 可ㄎㄜˇ
行ㄒ一ㄥˊ的ㄉㄜ˙方ㄈㄤ法ㄈㄚˇ告ㄍㄠˋ訴ㄙㄨˋ我ㄨㄛˇ如ㄖㄨˊ何ㄏㄜˊ做ㄗㄨㄛˋ， 不ㄅㄨˊ要ㄧㄠˋ
一ㄧˋ直ㄓˊ問ㄨㄣˋ我ㄨㄛˇ為ㄨㄟˋ什ㄕㄣˊ麼ㄇㄜ˙不ㄅㄨˋ這ㄓㄜˋ麼ㄇㄜ˙做ㄗㄨㄛˋ。

要做任何事，請先提醒我，讓我有段緩衝時間再去做。提醒我要把注意事項或應帶物品寫下來，讓我完成一項勾一項。

上課時我想走動，老師會用「有問題要問老師嗎？」來提醒我。我想一想好像沒有問題，只好走回座位坐下。

班規裡最好有一條：「上課管自己，有事老師會處理。」才不會讓大家亂告狀！

我們的班級公約

1. 上課眼睛看老師。

2. 上課管自己，有事別人會處理。

老師

找ㄓㄠ回ㄏㄨㄟˊ注ㄓㄨ意ㄧ力ㄌㄧˋ，才ㄘㄞˊ有ㄧㄡˇ上ㄕㄤˋ課ㄎㄜˋ權ㄑㄩㄢˊ！

給教師及家長的話

　　有的種子撒下後會很快開花，有的會慢點開花，有的則不開花，但可能會是一棵大樹。我們應該堅持給每個孩子獨特的機會，別太早為孩子下結論！

　　注意力缺陷過動症的孩子在高中職以下教育階段的特殊教育情緒行為障礙類別中，約占 83 ％，在正常孩子的出現率約占 3～7 ％。他們從小就像身上裝了馬達一般，總是沒定性，討厭需要輪流或等待的活動，在任何情境都可以過度的跑來跑去或爬上爬下，是教師們在班級經營上的頭疼對象！但事實上，資賦優異與注意力缺陷過動症的孩子幾乎都同樣有精力旺盛的特質，但為何資賦優異的孩子背後總站著驕傲的父母，而注意力缺陷過動症孩子的父母則總是恨不得將孩子藏起來？我想最大的差別就在於是否能集中注意力。資賦優異的孩子精力旺盛，但能集中注意力，所以會有好的各項成就；注意力缺陷過動症的孩子精力旺盛，但卻無法集中注意力，各項成就均落後，所以會使身旁的人不確定他們的未來。因此，「如何找回注意力」成為本書的重點！

　　如何協助注意力缺陷過動症的孩子找回注意力，重點環繞在四項主要策略，亦即適時醫療介入、行為改變技術、固定運動習慣及應用膳食療養。《找回注意力》繪本即圍繞著這四項策略提出簡單、正向、清楚、可行的問題解決方法，並搭配《找回注意力：學習手冊》（手冊中的學習單也是針對前述四項策略來設計的），希望能真正協助父母、教師及同儕了解這些孩子，讓注意力缺陷過動症的孩子可以享受適性學習，找回注意力，找回上課權！

註：《找回注意力：學習手冊》可單獨添購，每本定價新台幣 50 元，意者請洽本
　　公司。

where is my Attention?

Written by Ying-Ru Meng & Wen-Yu Chou
Illustrated by Hui-Chen Chu
Translated by Arik Wu

Ever since I was born, it seemed that there had been a motor in my body. I could never sit still.

I hated any activities that required waiting and taking turns.

I could keep running here and there or climbing up and down anytime and anywhere. Wasn't I great?

When I was in class, I could play with anything at hand, such as my fingers or erasers. I always lost things that I needed in class. I spent almost two thirds of my time searching for things and trying to concentrate. Wasn't I cool?

I was born in the Year of Dog, so my mom nicknamed me "Jumpy Dog."

Every time I did something wrong, my teacher would send me to the school counselor, so we soon became friends.

The counselor told me not to forget about the original intention of learning and to get distracted by the things going on around me. She also told me that as long as I take proper medication, do exercise on a regular basis, eat the right food and always stay positive, I, too, could learn well and be focused.

I wanted to learn well and be focused, so mom took me to the Division of Child & Adolescent Psychiatry at a neighborhood hospital. Guessed I would soon be healthy, ha!

The doctor told me to take Smart Drug every morning to keep me focused in class. Mom told me it is just like people who are near-sighted need to wear glasses to see clearly.

After having the Smart Drug, I would usually be too full to have lunch, so mom would cook more for dinner or prepare some night snacks for me to binge on. Yummy as always!

In addition, to make sure that I was physically and mentally healthy, my teacher also asked me to do aerobic exercise every morning on a regular basis.

She said doing exercise in the morning could help me concentrate in class, while do-ing so in the afternoon would only make me stay up late watching soap operas.

The secret to keeping me focused also lies in the food I eat!

Please teach me the rules in a simple, clear, understandable, and effective way, instead of keep asking me why I don't do it that way.

Tell me what I need to do next in advance and remind me to write down the dos and don'ts and assignments. That way, I will be able to find out what is still not finished.

When I tried to walk around in the classroom during the lecture, the teacher would ask me if I had any questions.

I would stop to think for a while, and realize that I had no questions at all, and then I would go back to my seat.

Our Classroom Rules

your teacher

1. Be good. If anything happens in class. ~~others~~ will take care of it.

2. Look at your teacher when he/she is talking.

There better be a classroom rule that says if anything happens in class, your teacher will take care of it. Otherwise, students would just keep telling on one another to the teacher.

It's time for class~~

Finally, I realized that if I could concentrate on my study, I would be able to learn well!